MR. MEN
Making Music
Roger Hargreaves

Hello, my name is Walter. Can you spot me in this book?

Original concept by
Roger Hargreaves

Written and illustrated by
Adam Hargreaves

When Mr Funny announced that he was starting a band, everyone was very excited. They began practising for the audition at the end of the week.

Some of the Mr Men were very good at playing music.

Little Miss Twins played the double bass.

Mr Busy played the flute with his busy fingers.

And Mr Noisy played the trumpet.

Loudly. All week long.

You see, you need practice to learn to play
a musical instrument.

Lots of practice.

And then more practice.

Little Miss Trouble also wanted to play in the band.

However, the trouble with Little Miss Trouble was that she was not the sort of person who could be bothered learning to play an instrument properly.

Practising was far too much trouble for her.

She tried the piano, PLONK! PLONK! PLONK!

And gave up.

She tried the violin, SCREECH! SCREECH! SCREECH!

And gave up.

And she tried the French horn, PARP! PARP! PARP!

And gave up.

She could not play in time or in tune.

But Little Miss Trouble was determined to be chosen to play in the band.

That week, everyone else continued to practise for the audition.

Mr Nosey practised the cymbals

Painfully!

Mr Quiet practised the piccolo.

Quietly.

Mr Tickle practised the trombone.

In a tangle!

Mr Nonsense practised the tuba.

In the bath!

And Little Miss Trouble did not practise at all.

Instead, she had a very busy night the night before
Mr Funny's audition.

A very busy night indeed!

A busy night making trouble.

First to audition the next day was Mr Cool with his saxophone.

He settled himself on the stage.

Mr Funny settled himself in anticipation.

Mr Cool took a deep breath.

He blew into his saxophone.

And a shower of water blew out of the saxophone into the air like a fountain.

Someone had filled his saxophone with water.

Mr Funny smiled.

Now, I am sure you can guess who that someone was!

And so the auditions continued.

Each new contestant met with a new disaster.

Little Miss Trouble had replaced the skin on Little Miss Bossy's drum with paper.

Mr Funny chuckled.

And she had swapped the strings on Little Miss Fun's guitar with spaghetti.

And Mr Funny laughed.

Then it was Little Miss Trouble's turn.

She felt very confident.

Nobody else had managed to play a note.

It did not matter how badly she played, she was bound to get into the band.

She stood in front of her xylophone, raised her arms and played.

PLINK! PLONK! BANG! BANG! PLINK! PLONK!

It was every bit as bad as you might imagine.

"That was very funny!" laughed Mr Funny. "I wasn't sure what sort of band it was going to be, but now I know. It is going to be a funny band and you will all be in it!"

And it was a very funny band.

What instrument do you think Mr Funny played?

The rubber band!